FLOWERFLOW
ED

Disney's
My Very First Winnie the Pooh™

Pooh's Mailbox

By Kathleen W. Zoehfeld   Illustrated by Mike Peterkin

SCHOLASTIC INC.
New York Toronto London Auckland Sydney
Mexico City New Delhi Hong Kong Buenos Aires

ISBN 0-7172-8922-2

12 11 10 9 8 7 6 5 4 3 2 1   1 2 3 4 5 6/0

Printed in the U.S.A.   56

First Scholastic printing, September 2001

Pooh peeked out the window. "I wonder if anyone has sent me a letter!" he thought. He sang a little on-the-way-to-the-mailbox song:

> *On any day, you never know*
> *What lovely things it may bestow.*
> *Dum dee dum, rum-tum-tiddle-um,*
> *I wonder what has come?*

"Oh," sighed Pooh, "it's nothing. Nothing is not a very exciting thing to get."

Pooh was wondering what to do next, when Piglet trotted up.

"Look what came in the mail!" Piglet cried, waving a set of instructions for haycorn planting.

"There was nothing in my mail," sighed Pooh.

"Would you like to share mine?" said Piglet.

"Oh, could I?" asked Pooh.

"Of course!" said Piglet.

FROM:
The Mastershalum Seed & Garden Supply Co.
Down Past the Floody Place

Growing an Oak Tree in Your Own Backyard

Instructions:

Step 1. Dig a small hole.
(It would be very nice to have a friend help you with this.)

Step 2. Place haycorn in hole.

Step 3. Cover it over with earth and pat it down nicely.
If you are a very small animal, jump on it.

Step 4. Water it.

Step 5. Wait.
(It would also be very nice to have a friend help you with this.)

Together they dug a hole and planted a haycorn. Then Piglet jumped on it and Pooh watered it and they began step 5, which said "Wait."

Piglet was thinking this step wasn't much fun when Pooh suddenly said, "Let's go see if Tigger got anything in the mail today!"

"Just what I've been waiting for!" cried Tigger as they arrived.

"Us?" asked Piglet.

"No, this nifty game that was in my mailbox today," he said, ripping it open. "See?"

"How nice to get a game in the mail!" Pooh sighed wistfully.

How to play

All players begin at the Lost Place.

...turns rolling the die to ...es they

CHANGED YOUR MIND. GO BACK 2 SPACES.

Go LEFT? Go RIGHT? FIRST DECIDE THEN ROLL AGAIN.

CHANGED YOUR MIND. GO BACK 3 SPACES.

HIDE IN A HOLLOW LOG LOSE A TURN.

...URN.

START

LOST PLACE

Lost in the Forest

Tigger

Tigger's House

The Hundred-Acre Wood

The Bouncing Cat Toy Co.

ON THE ROCKY BANK
JUST SOUTH OF THE NORTH POLE

Piglet thought the game looked very confusing.

"Well . . . you probably want to have fun with your game now, so we'll just be on our way," Piglet said to Tigger.

"Wait!" cried Tigger. "Stay! This here game's wanting to be played!"

So Pooh and Piglet stayed. And they played.

But after Tigger won the game three times in a row, Pooh said, "Do you think Owl got anything in his mailbox today? Why don't we go see him."

"Dear me, three months!" fussed Owl, waving a letter.

"Three months till what?" asked Pooh, peering at the letter. Everyone but him seemed to have gotten something in the mail today!

"Not *till* anything, dear boy," said Owl. "My Uncle Clyde Owl and Aunt Tabitha Pussycat are coming to stay for three months. Oh! Did I tell you about their wedding . . .?"

Uncle Clyde,
Edge-of-the-Sand Island,
Fiji

Everyone nodded "yes."

"Owl," Pooh said quickly, before he told them all over again, "how would you like to come with us to Kanga and Roo's?"

"Oh, what a good idea!" said Owl. "I'd love to!"

"Come in," said Kanga. "You're just in time for oatmeal. My sister sent me a yummy recipe in the mail – all the way from Australia!"

Mrs Kangaroo
Menindee
New South Wales
Australia

My Dearest Sister,

How is that little nephew of mine? Hard to believe he'll soon be two years old! My Joey is already out of the pouch and bouncing off with his friends most of the day. He's a good eater though, and always comes home for his oatmeal. Here's my secret recipe. Thought little Roo might enjoy it.

MRS. KANGAROO'S SECRET OATMEAL

1 3/4 CUPS WATER

1/4 TEAS...

1 1/3 CU...

"Tiggers love oatmeal!" said Tigger. He took a large spoonful and worked his tongue around. Then he made a face and said, "I orgot. Ig-ers on't ove o-eel."

Kanga just smiled and turned to Pooh.

"Would you like honey or milk with yours, Pooh?" she said.

"May I have both, please?" said Pooh. If he wasn't getting mail himself, it was very nice to share the good things that came to others.

hanking Kanga and Roo for the oatmeal, they moved on. Soon the friends came upon Rabbit, who was reading a book.

"Hello, Rabbit," said Pooh. "Would you like to join us for a little walk?"

"I'm busy," replied Rabbit. "I must read this important book I received in the mail."

HOW TO ORGANIZE
JUST ABOUT ANYTHING

CONTENTS

Introduction

Chapter 1   Organizing an Expedition

Chapter 2   Setting Up a Search

Chapter 3   Planning the Perfect Party (or other fun event)

Chapter 4   Improving the Lives of Everyone Through Organization

Rabbit
der the Sandy Bank
Hundred-Acre Wood

Sender:
The Helpful Hare Press
Department of Self-Improvement
193 Warren St., New York, NY

"In your mail . . . today?" said Pooh. "I see. Well, we'll just go on to Eeyore's, then."

"You're *all* going to Eeyore's?" cried Rabbit. "That's not a 'little walk.' That's an expedition, and it needs to be organized!" He took out a pencil and paper. "Everybody choose a partner!"

As they came near Eeyore's place, they heard singing.

"Happy birthday to me. Dum dee dum dum dee dee . . . ," sang Eeyore.

"We just had your birthday a month ago, Eeyore. How can it be here again, already?" asked Rabbit in surprise.

"My brother sent me many happy returns of the day," said Eeyore. "They just came in the mail."

DEAR EEYORE,
A VERY HAPPY
BIRTHDAY!
AND MANY HAPPY RETURNS
OF THE DAY.
Your Loving Brother
SEYMOUR
PLEASE COME FOR A
VISIT ANYTIME. WOULD
LOVE TO HAVE YOU.

"What a nice thing to get in the mail," sighed Pooh. "Happy return-of-your-birthday, Eeyore!"

Then Rabbit organized them into a wonderful party to celebrate the return of Eeyore's birthday. Eeyore had so much fun at his party that when everyone went home, he fell asleep right where he was!

Next morning, as soon as he got up, Pooh peeked out at his mailbox.

"Could *today* be the day I get something in *my* mailbox?" he wondered. And he sang:

> On any day, you never know
>
> What lovely things it may bestow.
>
> Dum dee dum, rum-tum-tiddle-um,
>
> I wonder if something has come . . . .

And something had!

Pooh got this from Piglet:

Thank you!

Dear Pooh,
Thank you for helping me plant my haycorn. It will be fun watching our oak tree grow together.
Love
Your best friend,
Piglet (me) xxx

POOH
under the name of Sanders
The Hundred-Acre Wood

And this from Tigger:

Dear Pooh
Please come to
Tigger's House to
play Lost in the Forest.
Come in the morning.
Love and bounces,
                    Tigger
P.S. Don't get lost
      on the way!

Pooh
under the name
     of Sanders
The Hundred-
Acre Wood

This came from Owl:

Dear Pooh,
Thank you for being there in my hour of need. I've thought it over calmly and decided a visit from Uncle Clyde Owl won't be so bad after all.
  I look forward to introducing him and Aunt Pussycat to you and all my other friends from the Hundred-Acre Wood.
      Sincerely Yours,
          Owl

Pooh
under the name
of Sanders
the Hundred-Acre
Wood

There was a note from Eeyore . . .

And there was an invitation to come to another birthday party!

"Oh, my!" thought Pooh. "Perhaps a full mailbox was worth waiting for, after all!"

an invitation:

Birthday Party!
Birthday Party!

<u>WHO</u>: Little Roo
<u>WHERE</u>: Roo's house
(Across from the Sandy Pit)
<u>WHEN</u>: 5·00 pm today
<u>RSVP</u>: Kanga

<u>P.S.</u> And Rabbit is organizing it so be there at 5·00 sharp!

Rabbit

Pooh

under the name
of Sanders

The Hundred-Acre
Wood